MW01178745

Katharine the Almost Great

Hair's Looking at You

by Lisa Mullarkey
illustrated by Phyllis Harris

magic
wagon

visit us at www.abdopublishing.com

To my own Goldilocks and Red-Headed Monkey Boy: I heart both of you! —LM
To Brandi, the best hairdresser around!—PH

Text by Lisa Mullarkey
Illustrations by Phyllis Harris
Edited by Stephanie Hedlund and Rochelle Baltzer
Interior layout and design by Jaime Martens
Cover design by Jaime Martens

Library of Congress Cataloging-in-Publication Data
Mullarkey, Lisa.
  Hair's looking at you / by Lisa Mullarkey ; illustrated by Phyllis Harris.
    p. cm. -- (Katharine the Almost Great)
  Summary: Katharine does not want to cut her long hair and donate it to
Locks of Love, but she is feeling pressured by the other girls in her third
grade class to do it--will she give in or stay true to herself?
  ISBN 978-1-61641-833-5
  1. Haircutting--Juvenile fiction. 2. Peer pressure--Juvenile fiction. 3.
Schools--Juvenile fiction. [1. Haircutting--Fiction. 2. Peer pressure--Fiction.
3. Schools--Fiction.] I. Harris, Phyllis, 1962- ill. II. Title. III. Series:
Mullarkey, Lisa. Katharine the almost great.
  PZ7.M91148Hai 2012
  813.6--dc23
                                          2011026388

MidAmerica11-13/1895

❋ CONTENTS ❋

❀ CHAPTER 1 ❀

A Hairy, Scary Decision

The smell of Mom's berrylicious pancakes drifted into my room. I jumped out of bed and raced down to the kitchen. "Do I smell blueberry pancakes?"

"And strawberry," said Mom.

Crockett yawned. Then he made a face at me. A not-so-nice face. "What's that?" he asked.

I snatched one of Jack's Tasty O's off of his tray. "What?"

"That!" he said as he poked my head.

I brushed my hand against my hair. It was squishy. Squashy. An ooey, gooey, chewy mess.

I gasped. "Oh no. It's . . ." I zipped my lips. The g-word makes Mom's voice thundery.

Dad leaned over. "I think it's . . ." Then he snapped his mouth shut and shook his head. Dad didn't want to say the g-word either.

So Crockett said it. "Gum."

I was doomed. Doomed!

Mom waved her spatula in the air. "*Gum?* Katharine Marie Carmichael, you know better than to chew gum in bed. You'd think after *last time . . .*"

Last time was when I was six. My babysitter let me practice my bubble blowing. The more gum I chewed, the bigger the bubbles. But that was the problem. My bubbles were *too* big.

They pop, pop, popped in my hair. My babysitter had to give me a haircut. The worst-haircut-in-the-history-of-the-world kind of haircut.

Mom lifted the tangled mess and sighed. "You never listen, Katharine."

"But I *do*," I insisted. "Remember when you said not to throw pennies into the fish fountain?"

She nodded.

"Well, I didn't!"

Mom raised her eyebrows. "But you threw *quarters* instead."

I sunk down in my chair and tap, tap, tapped my fingers. "At Tamara's sleepover, you told me not go to bed at midnight, didn't you?"

Mom nodded again.

"I listened. We went to bed at *twelve thirty!*"

Crockett rolled his eyes. "That's worse. She meant not to stay up late."

I rubbed my hands together. "Aha!" I said a minute later. "Didn't you tell me I'd become a couch potato if I watched too much TV? But I'm not a couch potato, am I? I sit on the floor."

Dad laughed. "So you're a *floor* potato."

I cleared my throat. "Did you know that the average kid spends 900 hours a year in school but watches over 1,500 hours of TV?" My calendar of useless facts sure comes in handy.

Mom wasn't impressed. "*Try* to be a better listener. Please."

I smooshed the blueberries with my fork. Then I shoved my plate to the side. My parents call me Katharine the *Almost* Great. They say I'm a work-in-progress. Maybe if I'd be a better listener, they'd call me Katharine the Great.

Dad scooped Jack out of his chair. He swooshed him through the air like Super Baby. Jack reached down and yanked my hair.

"Ouch!"

Jack giggled.

It was not a giggle moment.

Mom pulled scissors out of the drawer.

I covered my hair with a napkin. "Nope. No way."

"Just the sticky part," said Mom.

"But that's in the *middle* of my head," I said. "The only way you can get to the middle is to cut the bottom first."

"Try peanut butter," said Aunt Chrissy. "Rub it in and comb it out."

Mom frowned. "We're out of peanut butter." She glanced at the clock. "If we don't cut it out, you'll have to go to school like that." She inspected my hair again. "You could use a haircut."

Aunt Chrissy agreed. "Short hair's in. Even Penelope Parks has short hair now."

My mouth fell open. "Ewww. No way! If she had short hair, I'd know about it. After all, I'm her number one fan."

Aunt Chrissy fluff-a-puffed her hair. "I happen to love short hair."

"My mom's right," said Crockett. "It was on the news last night." He ran downstairs and got Aunt Chrissy's laptop. "Here," he said as he put it on the table. "Look it up."

Five seconds later, I was on Penelope's Web site. There was a picture of her holding her cut-off ponytail! The headline said: Teen Idol Donates Hair to Locks of Love. Click here for interview.

I clicked.

A bald man with a bow tie held a microphone in front of Penelope's smiling face. "How do you feel about donating your hair to Locks of Love, Penelope?"

Penelope blew a kiss to the camera. "It's for a great cause, dah-ling. My fans know I shine and sparkle on the *outside*. When they hear I've donated my hair to help others, they'll realize I shine and sparkle on the *inside,* too." Then she batted her eyelashes quicky quick. "If you want to shine and sparkle on the inside, donate *your* ponytail today."

Then Penelope grabbed the microphone from Mr. Bow Tie Man. "Be sure to visit my Web site for information on Locks of Love. After you get your hair cut, buy my new Razzle Dazzle Shampoo. It adds that extra bounce that short hair needs. At only $4.99 each, you'll be glad you did!"

Then she held up a bottle of the shampoo. "Remember, ounce for ounce, you'll get more bounce!" After blowing one last kiss to the camera, the interview ended.

Razzle Dazzle Shampoo? I had to have it!

"Maybe I'll donate *my* hair to Locks of Love. Then I'll buy Penelope's super-duper shampoo."

"That's expensive shampoo," said Mom. "Too expensive for us."

"But ounce for ounce, you'll get more bounce," I repeated. I didn't know exactly what that meant. But if Penelope said it, it had to be true.

Dad poured himself a cup of coffee. "If you're donating for the right reasons, go for it. But if you're donating because Penelope told you to, don't do it."

Aunt Chrissy gathered my hair and held it on top of my head. "You'd look cute with short hair."

We shuffled into the hallway so I could take a sneak peek in the mirror.

My stomach did a flip-flop belly drop.

I had a decision to make.

An important decision.

A very important hairy, scary decision.

❀ CHAPTER 2 ❀

On Your Mark, Get Set, Cut!

"You're really going to school with gum in your hair?" asked Crockett as we walked up the path.

I whipped out my glittery pink hat from my backpack and plopped it on my head. "Nope. I'm covering it up. No one will ever know."

"Mrs. Bingsley will know," said Crockett. "She knows everything."

He was right. Mrs. Bingsley mentioned the hat right away. "Katharine, that's a lovely hat. But hats belong outside. Please take it off."

I shook my head. "Can't."

"Can't?" asked Mrs. Bingsley. "Or won't?"

My shoulders went up and down. "I sorta kinda need to keep it on."

Vanessa had a goof-a-roo grin on her face. "Did you get a funny haircut?"

"Nope. No haircut."

"Did you color it orange again?" asked Tamara.

I put my hands on my hips. "My mom only lets me do that on Halloween."

"Do you have *bugs* in your hair?" asked Johnny.

"Ewwww," said Vanessa. "That's gross."

I put my hand on my forehead and used my best Penelope voice. "I would simply faint if I had creepy crawlies in my hair." My head itched just thinking about it.

Then Johnny plucked the hat off of my head. "She must have bugs!"

Everyone laughed.

Everyone but me.

I wanted to say:

"Johnny Mazzaratti, the only creepy crawly thing in this room is you. If you were a fly, I'd swat you."

But I didn't.

"It's just gum," I whispered. "G-U-M." I snatched my hat from Johnny and pulled it down over my ears.

Mrs. Bingsley patted my shoulder. "Olive oil will get that out." She reached into her desk drawer and handed me a comb. "It's left over from picture day. After lunch, ask your mom for some oil. During recess, I'll help you get the gum out." Then she turned to Johnny. "I'll see you at recess, too. You'll need to write Katharine an apology."

After lunch, I went into the kitchen to get oil. I also got an extra cookie.

"Why don't you wait until you're home, Katharine?" asked Mom. "Mrs. Bingsley shouldn't have to do this."

"She wants to help," I said. "You know what she always says."

Mom looked confused. "What?"

"That we're a caring community. We should help each other," I said and smirked. "Tsk, tsk. If *you* were a good listener . . ."

Mom laughed. She glanced at the clock. "Scoot! I need to work. *You* need to get that gum out."

Mrs. Bingsley was sitting at her desk grading papers when I went back to the room. Johnny was writing his note.

"Make it a good one," I said. But, I wasn't mad anymore.

I slid the cup of oil over to Mrs. Bingsley. She poured a few drops of oil onto my gunky spot. Then she glided the comb down my hair. "How many pieces of gum is this?" she asked. "Six?"

Mrs. Bingsley was one smart cookie! "How did you know?"

"A fellow gum chewer always knows," said Mrs. Bingsley. "I used to chew ten pieces at once."

"*Ten*?" asked Johnny.

"Wow!" I said. Then I got a hunch. "Did you have listening problems, too?"

"Yep," said Mrs. Bingsley. "All third graders do from time to time. Third grade is all about learning. We all make mistakes, but if we learn from them, we'll turn out alright in the end. I did. You will, too."

I heart Mrs. Bingsley!

Ten minutes later, presto change! The gum was gone. But now I smelled like icky salad.

"It's better than having bugs," said Johnny.

Mrs. Bingsley and I scritch scratched our heads.

After recess, the kids came back to the classroom. Everyone but Rebecca.

I pointed to the empty seat. "Where's Rebecca?"

The door opened. "I'm right here." She walked into the room wearing a blue hoodie. It almost covered her eyes.

"Rebecca went home for lunch," said Mrs. Bingsley. "She has a special announcement."

Rebecca held up a newspaper article. "Penelope Parks donated her hair to Locks of Love on Saturday."

The girls gasped when they saw Penelope's short hair.

Then Rebecca pulled off her hoodie.

Rebecca had short, short hair! Barely there hair.

She opened her bag and pulled out her ponytail. "I'm donating my hair, too!"

Everyone clapped and cheered.

"My aunt owns Shear Expectations. After lunch, I got my hair cut there." She ran her fingers through her hair. "Penelope was right. Short hair is extra bouncy."

"What's Locks of Love?" asked Diego.

"It's an organization that makes wigs out of human hair for kids who are sick. Sick enough that they've lost their own hair. My ponytail will be put together with other ponytails and will become a hairpiece."

Vanessa rushed up to see the picture of Penelope. "She looks pretty! So do you, Rebecca. Your hair is bouncy." Then she looked at the ends of her hair. "I'm going to get my hair cut, too."

"My aunt said she'll give anyone who donates to Locks of Love a free haircut," said Rebecca. "Her store is open until nine o'clock every night."

Vanessa jumped up and down like she was on a trampoline. "I'm going to make an appointment as soon as I get home. By tomorrow, I'll have bouncy hair, too."

"I can't wait," said Elizabeth.

"I hope my hair's long enough," said Caroline.

"I donated my hair in kindergarten," said Julia. "I'll do it again."

The room buzzed with excitement.

I didn't buzz about anything. Instead, I put my head on my desk and squeezed my eyes shut.

"What's wrong?" whispered Crockett. "Do you have a headache?"

I ignored him. Why? Because I didn't have a headache.

I had a hairache.

❀ **CHAPTER 3** ❀

Cut That Out!

When I got home from school, I headed straight to the kitchen. Mom's kiss cookies would cheer me up. I plucked three off of the plate.

Aunt Chrissy wrinkled her nose. "Something smells odd."

Mom sniffed Jack's diaper. "He's fine."

Aunt Chrissy scanned the kitchen. "It smells like an Italian hoagie."

"Or a salad?" I asked. "It's me and my oily hair."

"No more gum!" said Aunt Chrissy. "That's good! Oil did the trick?"

"Mrs. Bingsley helped me," I said. "But now I have a hairache."

Mom smiled as she lifted my chin. "Promise me no more gum before bed."

"Cross my heart promise," I said. "And I don't think I'll be eating salad for a long time."

Crockett stuffed a cookie into his mouth. "Tell them about Rebecca's hair."

"I saw it," said Mom. "I was in the hallway with Mrs. Ammer when Rebecca came back to school. She taught us a lot about Locks of Love."

Aunt Chrissy looked surprised. "First Penelope. Now Rebecca?"

"All the girls in our class are doing it," said Crockett. "Right, Katharine?"

I wanted to tell them that I wasn't so sure. But before I could, Mom gave me a great big hug-a-rooni. "So you made your decision? I'm so proud of you, Katharine! It's a very giving thing to do. Mrs. Ammer wants to start a Locks of Love program at our school."

My hairache just got worse. Mucho mega worse. "She does?"

"Not only that," said Mom, "she's also thinking of having an assembly about it. Maybe the newspaper will come. They might take pictures of all the girls who donated their hair to the program."

"I'll have a famous niece," said Aunt Chrissy.

Famous schmamous, I thought. When I walked into the hallway, I saw my reflection in the mirror. I got that icky feeling again.

When I got to school the next day, everyone was crowded around the swings. Crockett and I pushed through the crowd.

"It looks amazing," said Julia.

"You look pretty," said Rebecca. "Just like Penelope."

"I can't believe you did it," said Diego. "I liked your long hair better."

That's when I saw Vanessa. Now she had barely there hair, too!

"Do you like it, Katharine?" She shook her head from side to side. "Last night at dinner, I told my parents about Locks of Love. I wasn't sure I wanted to do it. But after watching Penelope's interview, I knew I had to. She was right! I feel shiny on the inside."

"It looks good," I said. "You just look . . . different."

Vanessa twirl-a-whirled around the playground. "Of course I look different! I have short hair now. When I got home, my parents bought me Razzle Dazzle Shampoo. Can you tell I have extra bouncy hair?"

I smiled, but I wanted to bounce myself home.

"My aunt gave me posters to hang around the school," said Rebecca. "Want to help, Vanessa?"

Rebecca grabbed Vanessa's hand as they walked away.

During the announcements, Mrs. Ammer read Vanessa's and Rebecca's names on the loudspeaker. They were lucky ducks.

I wanted to be a lucky duck. I wanted my name on the loudspeaker.

Everyone fussed over them.

I wanted everyone to fuss over me.

At eleven o'clock, Mrs. Curtin walked in. She had on her bunny slippers.

"Can anyone come to my classroom at twelve thirty each day this week? My kindergartners need help with a few projects."

Almost everyone's hands shot into the air.

Mrs. Bingsley pointed to our schedule on the board. "Don't forget that twelve thirty is your recess time."

All hands flew back down.

All except mine and Tamara's.

Mrs. Curtin gave us two thumbs-up. "Thanks so much, girls. I'll see you then."

A minute later, Vanessa tossed a piece of paper on my desk.

We're talking about Locks of Love at recess. Tell Mrs. Curtin you can't help her today.

I threw a note back.

I want to help the little kids. And Mrs. Curtin.

Vanessa scrunched her nose and scribbled fast.

But Locks of Love is important. Very, very important.

I tossed back another note.

Mrs. Curtin has helped me a lot in math. Now I want to help her. Helping Mrs. Curtin is very, very, VERY important. More important than a haircut.

Vanessa didn't throw another note back. She stuck out her tongue at me!

Miss Priss-A-Poo could be so rude!

At twelve thirty, while everyone played four square and rode scooters outside, Tamara and I helped Mrs. Curtin inside. We helped the kids sort colors, fold papers into different shapes, and practice counting from one to ten in Spanish.

After a half hour, Mrs. Curtin thanked us. "Your help means a lot to these kids. Thanks for donating your time."

Tamara and I skipped back to class.

"Are you getting your hair cut?" asked Tamara.

I shrugged. "I think so. Maybe." I chewed on my fingernail. "I'm not sure yet. Are you?"

Tamara ran her fingers through her hair. "It's too short. But yours isn't. It's extra long and extra pretty."

"Thanks," I said. *That's why I want to keep it.*

Every last inch of it.

Shear Expectations

The next morning, there was an even bigger crowd by the swings.

Someone was waving a stick in the air. I crept over to take a sneak peek. Vanessa and Rebecca were on the swings waving rulers. Oodles and oodles of girls surrounded them.

I was just about to leave and play four square with Crockett when Vanessa saw me.

"Katharine! Look what we have." She held up a ruler.

Rebecca jumped off of the swing and ran toward us.

"My aunt made these last night. Want one?" Rebecca asked.

She shoved a ruler in my hand. It said Shear Expectations ♥ Locks of Love. I handed it back. "I don't get it. Why rulers?"

"To let kids know that they'll need at least ten inches of hair from tip to tip to donate," said Rebecca. "We can measure everyone's hair at recess. We'll let them know if they have enough hair to donate."

Vanessa held up a ruler next to my hair. "Wow! You have at least fifteen inches! That would make a great hairpiece for someone." She looked over a list of names on a clipboard. "I don't see your name on this list. Are you donating your hair?"

I pushed Vanessa's hand away. "I'd be bald if I got fifteen inches of hair cut off."

Vanessa huff-a-puffed her cheeks. "You don't *have* to donate fifteen inches." She put the ruler up to my head again. "If you donated ten inches, your hair would be just below your ears."

"When are you signing up?" asked Rebecca.

I didn't want to answer. "Did you know that hair is made up of keratin?" I held out my hands and wiggle waggled my fingers. "It's in your fingernails, too."

"Who cares?" said Vanessa. "Are you donating your hair or not? You want to shine on the inside, don't you? Penelope said that you *have* to donate if you want people to know you shine and sparkle inside."

Tamara chimed in. "Of course Katharine's donating her hair. Right, Katharine?"

I looked at the list. It was a million miles long. Everyone waited for my answer.

This is what I wanted to say:

"I don't think so. I think it's great that you're doing it but I don't want to. Maybe I'll do it next year. Or in five years. But I can't do it now. I just can't."

But this is what I really said:

"Sign me up! Of course I want people to know I shine and sparkle on the inside." I had a lump in my throat. "Can't wait."

But I could wait. Forever and ever.

I was happy when the morning bell rang. I skedaddled inside as fast as I could.

But I wasn't happy for too long.

Mrs. Ammer announced five more names over the loudspeaker. They were second graders.

"Isn't it wonderful that second graders are also donating their hair?" said Mrs. Bingsley. "This really is such a caring community."

I felt guilty. Guilty with a capital G.

And it got worse! Mrs. Ammer visited our class.

"I have exciting news," she said. "The newspaper wants to write an article about Locks of Love. I thought they could interview you, Rebecca. You could tell them about your aunt, too. They'd like to take pictures."

Rebecca struck a silly pose. "Can they take a picture of Vanessa, too?"

"What a great idea," said Mrs. Ammer. "Maybe we'll ask them to come in next week and take a group shot of everyone who donated their hair."

"We should take before and after pictures of the girls," said Mrs. Bingsley.

"Maybe the after picture could show the girls holding their ponytails."

"And any boy who donates," said Crockett.

"Boys?" said Vanessa. "What boys?"

"Christopher Jenkins," said Crockett. "He's that kid in fifth grade with the long hair. Someone said he's donating his hair, too."

"The more the merrier," said Mrs. Ammer. "What a great idea. We could show all the pictures at our next character education assembly. After all, donating your hair to help others does show good character."

By the time Mrs. Ammer left, it was lunchtime.

"Can we *not* talk about Locks of Love?" asked Johnny at the lunch table.

"I agree," said Matthew. "Anything else but that."

Vanessa and Rebecca looked surprised. "We like talking about it, don't we Katharine?"

"I do," said Tamara. "But I agree. "Let's talk about the new basketball hoops we're getting on the playground."

And we did.

Instead of going to recess, Tamara and I went back to Mrs. Curtin's class.

"It's so good to see both of you," said Mrs. Curtin. "We're working on adding details to our drawings." She handed us each a stack of pictures.

Easy breezy!

I held up a picture of a flower.

"That's mine," whispered Sarah Parker.

Sarah was a cutie pie. She had on a striped dress with little flowers on her leggings. A matching headband kept her hair out of her face.

She grabbed my hand and led me to the carpet. We ploppity plopped on beanbag chairs and got comfy cozy. "I like your flower," I said.

But I didn't *really* like her flower. It didn't have leaves. Or color. It was as plain as vanilla ice cream. "Why don't you color in your flower?"

"Can I use pink?" she asked. "It's my favorite color."

"I like pink, too," I said. We colored it in together.

"Look at the flower on Mrs. Curtin's desk," I said. "What do you see at the bottom?"

Sarah studied the flower. "Leaves!"

After she added three leaves, she added birds, clouds, and grass to her picture.

I looked over her picture. "I love it! You added such great details."

Next, I worked with Lea, Emmie, Jose, and Megan.

"Time's up," said Mrs. Curtin. "Again, I can't thank you girls enough for donating your time. It's so generous of both of you."

If only I felt generous with my hair.

❀ CHAPTER 5 ❀

Kids Care Club

I was crank, crank, cranky walking to school the next day. "I think I might go home sick."

"What's wrong?" asked Crockett.

"Hearing the announcements is going to cause me barf-a-rama Locks of Love drama."

Crockett laughed.

"It's not funny, Crockett. Can I tell you a secret? A super-duper-you-can't-tell-anyone secret?"

He nodded.

"I don't want to donate my hair."

"Then don't," said Crockett.

"But everyone else is," I said. "It's not that I don't want to help people. I just don't want to help people by cutting my hair."

Crockett kicked a pebble. "If I had long hair, I'm not sure what I'd do."

My heart thumpity thumped. "Really, Crockett? Honest?"

"Scout's honor," he said.

I felt a teensy-weensy better.

I didn't say anything else until we got to school. As we unpacked our backpacks, Caroline and Elizabeth rushed through the door.

"We did it," said Caroline. She pumped her fist in the air. "I cut eleven inches off. Elizabeth cut off thirteen!"

I flashed them a fake smile as Vanessa fluttered by.

"Katharine! Why haven't you gotten your hair cut yet? Don't you want your name on the loudspeaker?" She folded her arms over her chest. "You can't join our club until you do."

That's when I noticed the pink bracelets Rebecca was handing out. "What club?"

"The Kids Care Club," said Vanessa. "The only way you can join is to donate your hair. Then you'll get one of our bracelets."

The bracelets were glittery. "Can I have one now?" I asked. "Please?"

Vanessa stuck her nose in the air. "Not until you get your hair cut."

"But I'm a caring kid," I whispered. "Aren't I?"

Vanessa spun around on her heel. "Rules are rules." She stomped away while fluff-a-puffing her hair.

Vanessa had a bad case of sassitude!

I wanted to pull her hair. But I didn't.

I decided not to think about the club for the rest of the day. But then Mrs. Bingsley let us have free reading time. When I asked Elizabeth to be partners, she jingle jangled her bracelet.

"Sorry. I can only read with girls who are in the club."

So I read alone.

During lunch, I asked Vanessa if she wanted to trade her banana for my apple. She loves apples!

"Sorry," said Vanessa. "You're not in the club." Then she picked up her tray and glided over to another table. A table packed with kids wearing pink bracelets.

I glared at Tamara. "Who cares about them? Let's go to Mrs. Curtin's class."

Tamara bit her lip. "Sorry. Can't. I'm helping Vanessa and Rebecca measure hair." She took a bracelet out of her pocket and slipped it on. "Since I can't donate my hair, they made me an honorary member."

I stomp, stomp, stomped all the way down to the kindergarten class.

"Where's Tamara?" asked Mrs. Curtin.

"Recess," I muttered.

"Well, I appreciate that you came, Katharine. I can always count on you." She handed me a book. "Just read to small groups today. Okay?"

I nodded.

But it's hard to read to a group of kids when two of them are wearing glittery pink bracelets.

When I finished, Mrs. Curtin walked me into the hallway. "Thanks again for donating your time, Katharine."

When the bell rang at the end of the day, Mom met me at my classroom. "Are you up for helping me in the cafeteria? I need to stay late and get things done. Aunt Chrissy's watching Jack, and Crockett has a Junior Rangers meeting." She waved to Mrs. Bingsley. "Since the teachers have a meeting across town, we'll have the whole place to ourselves."

All the girls were going to have their first club meeting at Vanessa's house. Guess who wasn't invited?

Me! That's who!

So while Mom scrubbed pots, I brought plastic forks and spoons to the teacher's room. Then I got to count the leftover milk and the lunch money in the cash register. Then we planned the menu for the next two weeks. Mom even agreed to make Strawberry Blasts one day.

At five o'clock, Mom looked at her watch. "We're almost done. I have to work in the freezer for ten minutes." She slipped on her coat, hat, and gloves. "I'll brave it alone if you bring that coffee pot down to the office. Put it behind Mrs. Tracy's desk." She held out her hand. "Deal?"

I shook her hand. "Deal."

I lugged the pot all the way to the office. "Hello?" I yelled when I opened the door. "Anyone here?"

Nobody answered.

I shoved the pot on the shelf and was about to leave when I saw it.

The loudspeaker!

I wasn't planning on pressing the big fat green button in the middle that said PRESS TO SPEAK.

But I did.

Nothing happened. My heart pounded as I pressed it harder this time. I leaned over the box and spoke into it. "This is Katharine Marie Carmichael. The most fab-u-lo-so third grader at Liberty Corner School."

My voice boomed throughout the hallways!

I pressed the button again and pretended I was Mrs. Ammer.

"Congratulations to all of the nice third graders. That would be Katharine Marie Carmichael. No one else. Except for her cousin, Crockett. Katharine is a very caring and charming child. But her classmates are not. Except for her cousin, Crockett. Miss Priss-A-Poo and Rebecca are bullies. And copycats. And meanies. Meanies with a capital *M*."

This was fun!

But the fun didn't last long.

I heard a door squeak. Creak. I thought it was Mom.

But it wasn't Mom.

It was Ammer the Hammer.

I got nailed!

❀ CHAPTER 6 ❀

Blow-by-Blow

"Feeling chatty this afternoon, Katharine?" asked Mrs. Ammer. She had a frowny face. "Where's your mother?"

"I'm right here and about to crawl under a desk. I'm so embarrassed, Mrs. Ammer." She looked like a puffy snowman dressed in her winter clothes.

I glanced at Mrs. Tracy's desk. I wondered if there was room enough for two under it.

Mrs. Ammer took a deep breath. "Did you know that the loudspeaker is to be used by school employees only?"

They both stared at me with angry eyes and folded arms.

I sucked in my breath. "Did you know that most foods freeze when the temperature is zero degrees Fahrenheit? Freezing makes the water in the food turn to ice."

"Answer the question, Katharine," said Mrs. Ammer.

This is what I wanted to say:

"Of course I knew the loudspeaker was for school employees only. But my fingers didn't know that. They started going crazy and pressing buttons."

But this is what I really said:

"I'm really, really sorry, Mrs. Ammer. I came in to drop off that coffee pot and I saw all the buttons. I couldn't stop myself."

Mom's voice thundered. "You know you aren't to touch things that don't belong to you, Katharine. Why would you play with the loudspeaker?"

I didn't know what to say. I didn't know what to do.

A tear dripped. A tear dropped.

"Are you crying because you got caught?" asked Mrs. Ammer. "Or is there something else wrong?"

Salty tears poured down my cheeks. "Both."

Mom handed me a tissue. "Start at the beginning, Katharine. Tell us everything. Then maybe we'll be able to understand why you said those mean things about Vanessa and Rebecca."

"You heard that?" I cried harder.

Mom nodded. "The freezer has a speaker."

I groaned. I moaned. Then I told them all about my hairy, scary decision.

"Why didn't you just say you didn't want to do it?" asked Mrs. Ammer.

"I tried," I said. "But I felt like Vanessa and Rebecca bullied me. They said *everyone* was donating hair. Then they wouldn't let me join their club."

"Club?" said Mrs. Ammer. "What club?"

"The one where all the members get to wear those pinklicious bracelets. They named it the Kids Care Club. You can't be a member unless you donate your hair to Locks of Love." I lowered my head. "I'm not a club member."

"But you're a very caring kid!" said Mrs. Ammer. "Wasn't it your idea to collect pennies for the needy?"

I nodded.

"And aren't you giving up recess to help Mrs. Curtin's class?"

I nodded again. "I wanted to help Mrs. Curtin."

"Do you know why you wanted to help Mrs. Curtin?" asked Mrs. Ammer. "Because you're a caring kid."

Mom's voice was normal again. "Why didn't you tell me you were having second thoughts? I certainly didn't expect you to cut your hair."

"But you seemed so excited," I said. "I didn't want to let you down. Everyone was making such a big deal about Locks of Love."

"Well," said Mrs. Ammer, "it is a big deal. It's a great organization that helps lots of kids. But perhaps we focused too much on it. Maybe we got a bit too excited about the newspaper coming."

"I know a lot of kids did it for the right reason," I said. "But some kids did it for the wrong reason. They donated their hair just because Penelope donated hers. I almost did that. But my dad said that wouldn't be the right reason."

Mrs. Ammer smiled. "I agree with your dad, Katharine. And you know what? I'm glad you're not getting your hair cut."

"Really?" I asked. "Why?"

"Because you did what *you* wanted to do. Not what others wanted you to do. That's not always an easy thing." She gave my shoulders a little squeeze-a-roo. "How about I forget that I heard anything over the loudspeaker as long as you promise never to touch it again?"

"That's the best idea I've heard all day," I said.

And it was, until I heard my dad's super-duper idea after dinner. "Why don't we go celebrate by getting ice cream at the Polar Cub?"

"What are we celebrating?" I asked.

"You being true to yourself, Katharine. If you ever decide to donate your hair, we'll support you. But we also support your decision now. We're glad you didn't do it just to go along with the crowd."

"Or to get in the club," added Crockett.

Mom sneezed. "Since it's only fifty degrees outside and I'm still chilled to the bone from the freezer today, you celebrate without me."

"Do you need some tissues?" I asked.

Mom laughed. "Katharine, you really are a caring kid."

I was a caring kid! I felt all warm and fuzzy inside *and* outside. And I didn't have to choppity chop my hair off to feel that way.

A Lesson Learned

When Mrs. Bingsley greeted us at the door the next morning, she had a scarf wrapped around her head.

"Did you get your hair cut for Locks of Love?" asked Vanessa.

"Her hair isn't long enough to donate," I said. Then I slathered my lips with Luscious Lemon Lip Gloss. "Oh, and by the way, Vanessa, I'm not donating my hair. Maybe I will next year."

Vanessa covered her mouth with her hand.

"And that doesn't mean I'm not a caring kid," I said. "I just don't have to cut my hair to prove it."

Everyone stared at me.

My face felt like it was on fire. "Did you know that a woman in China holds the world record for having the longest hair? Her hair is over eighteen feet long!"

Before anyone could say anything else, Mrs. Bingsley rang the bell on her desk. "Can I have your attention? I have something to share."

Everyone quieted down and faced Mrs. Bingsley.

"After school yesterday, I spoke to my niece," said Mrs. Bingsley. "She told me that Penelope Parks has a new look."

"We know," said Vanessa. "She cut her hair. She has short and bouncy hair now."

"Another new look," said Mrs. Bingsley. "I went to her Web site. She looks very different. She said that if anyone wanted to have the coolest hair around, they'd have to color it."

Then Mrs. Bingsley unraveled her scarf. "So I did!"

Everyone gasped.

Mrs. Bingsley had blue hair! Bluer than blue hair.

"Do you like it?" she asked.

It looked disgust-o! But everyone nodded.

"Here's a picture of Penelope," said Mrs. Bingsley. "She's my inspiration." She pressed a button and Penelope's picture popped up on the whiteboard.

"If you go to her Web site, she has special shampoo just for girls and boys with blue hair. My niece is so excited. She started a new club and I'm allowed to join. It's a club for people who have blue hair."

Vanessa waved her hand in the air. "I want blue hair! I think it looks great! Can you tell me more about the club? I love clubs!"

Just then, Mrs. Curtin walked into our room. She had blue hair, too!

"Mrs. Bingsley! I didn't know you dyed your hair! I saw Penelope on the news last night. I knew I had to have hair like hers."

Some kids laughed. But not Rebecca. "I want to dye my hair, too. I'm going to ask my aunt if she can do it for me today."

Then the craziest thing happened. Most of the kids started to raise their hands and say that they wanted blue hair, too.

I didn't. Gross-a-rama!

And then Mrs. Ammer waltzed into the room. She had blue hair, too!

"Ladies! Did you happen to watch Penelope on the news last night?" asked Mrs. Ammer. "When I heard Penelope say that I had to color my hair to show others how much I really sparkle, I had to do it."

"Do you think I could dye my hair purple or pink instead?" asked Vanessa.

"Well, of course you can," said Mrs. Ammer. "But you won't be able to join our club."

Vanessa slumped down in her seat.

"That's right," said Mrs. Bingsley. "You have to do exactly what Penelope says to join the club. If you're not cool enough to dye your hair blue, well, then . . . sorry."

"Blue is fine," mumbled Vanessa.

But Vanessa didn't look fine. She had angry eyes. Watery eyes.

"I have another announcement," said Mrs. Bingsley. "I'm going to hang out with Mrs. Ammer and Mrs. Curtin today. They are, after all, the coolest people in this school according to Penelope. So you're getting a substitute. Make sure you're on your best behavior."

Johnny grumbled. "We don't like having substitutes."

"As soon as you all get your hair dyed blue, I'll come back," said Mrs. Bingsley. "But I only want to hang out with people who have blue hair."

Vanessa fiddled with her bracelet. "You liked teaching us all this year. You told us we were great kids. Just because we don't have blue hair doesn't mean we're not cool." Then Vanessa sucked in her breath. Her face turned red. Redder than red. She put her head on her desk and groaned.

"What's wrong, Vanessa?" asked Mrs. Curtin.

Vanessa sighed. "Penelope didn't dye her hair blue, did she?"

Mrs. Ammer smiled. "Nope. I photoshopped it."

"We didn't either," said Mrs. Curtin. "On the count of three . . . One . . . Two . . . Three."

When they all said three, they yanked the wigs off of their heads and threw them in the air.

"I don't get it," said Rebecca. "Why did you pretend Penelope said all that stuff? I was going to dye my hair tonight when . . ." She stopped talking. Her eyes lit up. "Oh, I get it now."

"I don't get anything," said Tamara. "What's going on?"

Mrs. Bingsley patted Tamara on the back. "Let's have Katharine explain it to everyone."

So I did.

" . . . and then I felt bullied into cutting my hair. I wanted to fit in so I almost did it. It hurt when everyone got pinklicious bracelets and I didn't. No one would let me join the Kids Care Club. But I'm glad I didn't get my hair cut. I'm just not ready." I turned to Vanessa. "But I show I care in other ways. Lots of other ways."

"Like the Penny Harvest," said Crockett.

"And thinking of the most per-fect-o Christmas present for me," added Mrs. Bingsley.

Mrs. Curtin stepped forward. "You may not have donated your hair, Katharine, but you donated your time to my class this week. That meant a lot to me."

Vanessa rushed over to me and gave me a ginormous hug. "I'm really sorry, Katharine. I'll never ever do anything like that again."

"Third grade is all about learning," said Mrs. Bingsley. "We all make mistakes, but . . ."

My eyes lit up. "But if we learn from them, we'll turn out alright in the end."

❀ CHAPTER 8 ❀

A Cut Above

That afternoon, we had a surprise assembly. When I walked down to the gym, Mrs. Ammer pulled me out of line.

"The newspaper's here, Katharine. I was wondering if you could talk to them."

"Me?" I asked. "About what?"

"About being true to yourself. About standing up for yourself and not going along with something just because everyone else does. About being brave."

"But I didn't feel brave," I said. "I almost cut my hair."

"But you didn't," said Mrs. Ammer. "And I think it's an important lesson for all of the students to hear."

I hoped Mr. Bow Tie Man interviewed me.

"They want to speak to you after the assembly. Will you do it?"

"Okeydokey, Mrs. Ammer. I can't wait."

The assembly was awesome. Rebecca's aunt came to speak about Locks of Love. "So far, I've had in sixty-seven kids from Liberty Corner School. Twenty-six more kids have signed up. There's even one boy who is coming in next week."

Everyone laughed.

Then Mrs. Ammer read the names of each person who donated hair. We clapped for each girl and boy when the before and after pictures flashed on the screen.

"While Locks of Love is certainly a way to show that you're a caring kid, it's not the only way," said Mrs. Ammer. "Other ways are when you participate in community service projects, say hello to people in the hallways, hold doors open for each other, and spend time with family and friends. Saying a kind word to someone who might need it shows you really care. How many of you have been kind and caring to someone this week?

Three hundred hands flew up into the air. I put up two.

"Starting this month," said Mrs. Ammer, "we're going recognize students for their kind and caring ways. If you see someone being kind to another person, I'd like to know about it." She held up a purple box and a stack of papers. "I'll have this box outside my office door. Fill out a form when you see someone being kind. Write the person's name and what they did to show kindness. Each day, I'll pick a few of them out of the box and read them over the loudspeaker."

My stomach did a flip-flop belly drop when she said the "L" word!

"Who knows," said Mrs. Ammer, "maybe I'll let some of you read the papers over the loudspeaker."

I heart Mrs. Ammer! I was pretty sure she meant me.

It was a per-fect-o day. And it got even better that night.

There was a knockity knock on my door after dinner.

It was Vanessa. "What are you doing here?" I asked.

"I wanted to apologize again. I feel awful about the whole club thing. And for being a bully about your hair." She pulled a package out from behind her back. "This is for you."

"Me?" I blushed. "Why?"

"I bought it for you the other day. But my mother didn't want me to bring it to school in case it spilled. Go ahead," she said. "Open it. It's just for being a friend."

I sniff, sniff, sniffed the bag. "It smells like raspberries."

Vanessa jumped up and down. "Open it faster. I know you'll love it."

And I did! It was Penelope Parks's Razzle Dazzle Shampoo.

"I love it, Vanessa. I'm a lucky duck!" I read the back. "Penelope said it's for short hair only."

Vanessa made a scrunchy face. "She also said that you had to donate your hair to show people you're shiny on the inside. We know that's not true."

"Can I ask you a question, Vanessa?" I said.

She ran her fingers through her bouncy hair. "Sure."

"Did you donate your hair because you really wanted to or because Penelope cut hers?" I asked.

"At first, I wanted to do it because of Penelope," said Vanessa. "But when I told my parents about Locks of Love, they told me about my Aunt Rose. She was sick when she was my age. She lost all of her hair. Her family didn't have money to buy her a wig. She had to go to school without one until her own hair grew back. Some kids teased her. After I heard the story, I knew I *had* to donate my hair. I wanted to."

"Wow, Vanessa. You really are a kind and caring kid."

And as soon as I got to school on Monday morning, I headed straight to the purple box. I wanted to make sure everyone else knew it, too.

Be a Caring Kid

Here are ten ways to sparkle and shine on the inside:

1. Collect food for your local food bank. Involve your whole school!
2. Grab some friends and sing your favorite songs at a nursing home.
3. Read a book to a friend or a favorite pet.
4. Visit an animal shelter and ask if you and an adult can volunteer.
5. Make and send cards to our military.
6. Write a thank-you note to someone.
7. Sell lemonade and cookies and donate your proceeds to a favorite charity.
8. Donate books you no longer read to someone who will enjoy them.
9. Bag all of the clothes you've outgrown and give them to a homeless shelter.
10. Be neighborly. Shovel your neighbor's sidewalk or weed their garden for free.